Maybe, a mole

Also by Julia Cunningham

MAYBE,
a mole

by Julia Cunningham

Illustrated by Cyndy Szekeres

Pantheon Books

141516171819

With love to
Fabio Coen
who walks so welcome in my
world of words
and to
Saul Fisher
who gave it greenness

Contents

A Different Treasure

hat foolishness," said the fox, his glinting look directed at the very small mole who was stretched as flat as a leaf on the summit of a boulder. "You belong underground and will fry your gizzard on that rock."

"That's what I'm hoping will happen," replied the mole in an almost vanished voice. "They don't want me down there."

"Indeed," said the fox. "And why not? Are you stupid—or perhaps unwilling to be moleish?"

"Not unwilling. Unable. I am different from the rest. I can see."

For the first time the fox's interest sharpened and he looked at the despairing animal with some respect. "And the others are quite naturally blind, is that not so?" he said. He smoothed his whiskers thoughtfully. "Why didn't you hide your unnatural ability?"

The mole raised his pointed head from the

stone. "I couldn't. I love to look." As he continued to talk he slowly sat up. "I would come out of a tunnel at sunset and let the sky dazzle me, then go back and tell them about the colors. I would pop up into a cornfield when all the corn was ripe and look at the stalks that columned the sky like

spires and go back and tell them about it. I would—"

"Yes, yes," said the fox. "Let's not cloud the problem with a description of a world I know very well. What happened, finally?"

"They held a meeting of all the hereabout moles, even called it an Assembly, and decided to banish me. They threw me out is how I feel about it. Might as well have simply shoved me from the burrow like a sack of bad roots. Even my brothers and sisters were too ashamed to say goodbye at the last."

The fox gazed impatiently at the mole who was now heaving softly with suppressed sobs. "Why don't you cry for a few minutes and get it over with? Then we can discuss how you can best serve me."

The mole lost his tears in astonishment. "Serve you? But why?"

"Because you need employment in an upper world where you are a stranger. Otherwise you will become a victim. Some other animal might make a slave of you forever, knowing your gentleness and inclination to please."

"You seem to know me very well already," said the mole shyly, rather comforted by the fox's understanding.

"I do, old friend, I do. I am not known to be brilliant for nothing." The fox dedicated an instant to pride then continued. "First I must know your name."

"It's Maybe."

The fox laughed. "May be, might be. Flay me, knight me!"

"No need to make fun," said the mole with some dignity. He had left the boulder and was seated in the grass under the partial shade of a dandelion.

"I'm not really. Rhymes come to me quite at random. However, to business, dear Maybe. Climb onto my shoulder. I wish to show you something."

The mole obeyed and found a cozy hollow in the soft, cinnamon fur.

"See that rather weary house over the hill?" asked the fox.

"I do," responded the mole looking intently at the uneven roof, the peeling paint, and the ragged, untended geraniums at each side of the cracked front door.

"It belongs to a most ungenerous man named Sting. He feeds his chickens so little they're not worth stealing. And he's never been known to give so much as a walnut to a hungry squirrel. Oh, he's happy enough. No need to crinkle up with pity. But the point is he is rumored to have buried a great treasure somewhere about his house. And that's where you come in. You're to dig for it."

"And if I find it?"

"We'll divide the gold. One share to you, nine shares to me."

"How do you know it is gold?" asked the

mole, unaware of the unbalanced bargain.

"I don't. But what else would be worth burying? How about it? Are you willing?"

"Maybe," said the mole.

"I already know your name," said the fox who, when he was determined, never accepted a weak reaction.

The mole smiled. "I'll do it," he said. "You're my friend and I'll do it."

So it was that that very evening, after the sunset had left the windows of Mr. Sting's house, Maybe began his methodical tunneling. First he circled the house under the earth, then foot by foot, widened his search. A little before midnight he emerged, very dirty and very tired.

The fox was waiting for him.

"No luck," said Maybe, "except some grubs I ate for my supper."

"No luck, no pluck," rhymed the fox. He saw his mistake in the hurt look of Maybe's eyes. "Oh, don't mind me," he added hast-

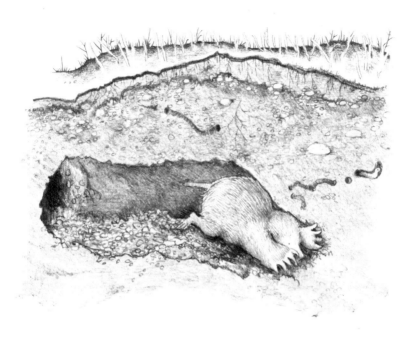

ily. He knew that Mr. Sting would see the
lines of humped earth around his house in
the morning and be on watch ever after for
the mole. This night was their only chance.

"I know what you're thinking," said
Maybe.

"Do you?" The fox was beginning to find
the mole his equal, if not in handsomeness
at least in intelligence and that, after all, was
of more value.

"Yes. And we've only a few more hours until sunrise so back I'll go."

All the rest of that night the mole kept bravely at his search. No matter that his paws were now so worn with digging that each advance brought further pain. No matter that his breathing was harsh and his back all one fiery ache. Round and round he went until a circle as wide as a small lake had been thoroughly burrowed. But he was no longer a mole alone. He had found a friend and he would do his best, as a friend should.

And halfway through his ordeal, when he emerged briefly for fresh air, he had found something. A small sack of seeds—flat, gray seeds. He had eaten a few for strength and then, to keep himself going, had tied the sack to his tail so he could occasionally halt to munch. But it was not until he was ready to go above ground at the end that he noticed the sack had emptied as he worked.

He disengaged his tail, resolving not to tell his disappointed comrade, and poked his head into the first shaft of the rising sun.

Just before him, almost scarlet in the new light of day, was the fox.

Maybe simply collapsed with only enough energy to shake his head sorrowfully before he fell into a profound sleep.

Gazing at this small creature who had so faithfully carried out his part of the bargain in spite of continuing discouragement, who had worked all night to please a partner who planned, if successful, to cheat him, the fox suddenly discovered who and what the mole was—someone to be trusted, to be company, to be loved.

Gently he lifted him to his back, never disturbing the rhythm of his sleeping, and set off for his den in the far woods.

From that day onward they shared their lives, each giving to each through the hard, cold winter that arrived too soon and stayed too long. Nor did they ever go back to Mr. Sting's property. The adventure had become a memory.

But one fine morning when the world had turned green again and the birds had returned to the trees, Maybe awoke with a smile and suggested a holiday. "And I'll show the way," he said.

"We'll never lose, if you choose," conceded the fox.

Maybe, quite used by now to his friend's glib way with words, led off, the fox patiently keeping behind the mole's slowness.

At last, at noon, they came to the border of Mr. Sting's land and suddenly they halted stock-still in their tracks.

No longer was the horizon bare of anything but grass. The whole hill was blazing with giant, yellow sunflowers. It was as though the sun itself had descended from the sky and chosen this field to visit.

Maybe gasped. The fox sat down hard on his haunches.

When he had recovered from the first shock of this glory Maybe told the fox about finding the seeds and what had happened.

"But, Maybe," said the fox, his eyes as bright as the flowers, "you did find it!"

The mole's mouth began to curve upward. "You mean the gold?" he said.

And suddenly, above the hum of the bees and the rustling of the air through the leafy stalks of the sunflowers, rose the high hilarity of their laughter. On and on it spiraled until they were both flat on their backs, holding their sides. And even that evening after they had eaten their supper and the darkness had come close to the entrance of their home, they had only to look at one another for the heaves of laughter to begin again.

The Ring of Roses

The first time Maybe met the mouse with the white ruff around his neck was in the lady's vegetable garden. The mouse was propped lazily up against a cabbage, whistling through his teeth.

He noticed the mole but went right on into the second chorus of *Cheese Is Here to Please.*

In the meantime, while waiting courteously to say good morning, Maybe looked at the mouse. The white ruff did indeed give his grayness a noble touch, and for such a small, pointy creature he might have been termed handsome. But there was a kind of arrogance in the way he was waving his paws in time to his own music that offended the usually very tolerant mole. It was as though he expected the whole world to halt and take notice.

The mole considered simply continuing on his way because something rather excit-

ing had happened and he wanted to tell his
friend and partner, the fox, about it without
delay. In his early-morning tunneling in the
lady's apple orchard he had found a ring,
a gold ring, engraved all around with tiny
roses. The mole had placed it into his left
cheek for safekeeping and even the flavor
of the metal seemed sweet.

He was just about to take his leave when
the mouse spoke. "You have enjoyed my
whistling, I'm sure."

18

Maybe, who preferred to be pleasant whenever possible, nodded.

"You may introduce yourself," stated the mouse.

"I am Maybe and I live just over the hill in a very snug den I share with the fox."

The mouse tried not to seem impressed but he rose from his lolling posture and stood up to the height of the row of young radishes to his left. "Indeed. I am Alfred, Master of the House."

"What house?" asked the mole, seeing only the great edifice that belonged to the lady who inhabited it all by herself and who was of no worry or trouble to those smaller than she. In the summer they were welcome to take a portion of her produce and if the winter was hard she put out turnips and onions and suet and stale bread for their needs. They knew they were secure from harm when she worked in her garden and even the rabbits nibbled close to her skirts.

"Surely," thought Maybe, "this little almost-nobody doesn't mean *her* house?" But he was wrong.

Alfred was pointing an imperious paw toward the weathered white rise of doors and windows and chimneys.

Maybe blocked a smile. "You are master of the mice of the house. How satisfactory."

"Not at all. Of the entire." His paw swept a line from cellar to attic.

"And the lady is in your service perhaps?" Very infrequently Maybe allowed himself a dash of irony.

The mouse stroked his tail idly as though his companion deserved little or no attention. "Not exactly," he mused. "She keeps things in order for me."

Keenly tempted to laugh, the mole instead burrowed his snout into the thick grass and kept it there until he could control his amusement. "Poor little mite," he murmured to himself. "No sense whatsoever."

But the mouse had caught the signals of doubt from the mole.

"I can prove it, if you wish. She built a small wooden house for me and it sits on the kitchen windowsill. It has five rooms, including an upstairs porch."

"A doll's house," said the mole privately.

"And each morning she asks me important questions like 'How is the weather going to be today?' and 'Do you think it is time to pick the tomatoes?'"

"And you tell her?"

"Naturally. She seems to understand my squeak-talk very well."

For an instant the mole wanted to enclose this deluded pity of a mouse in a tender hug, to give him the shelter of his affection, a moment of warmth before the great world cracked down on him. But in the next moment he found it easy to resist his impulse for Alfred had pranced over to him and was patting the mole's shoulder.

"We can't all occupy high positions," he was saying between pats. "Don't be downcast by your lowly role in life."

With a hurried goodbye Maybe scurried out of sight and hearing and then he tumbled himself into a clump of clover and laughed so heartily the ring slipped from his mouth. He lay there quietly for a few minutes gazing at the ring of roses. How very beautiful it was! And for the very first and last time he wished he might be a person so that he could wear it on a special finger. He was reminded of the conceit of the mouse, believing he controlled the doings of the lady and her house and he got up and ambled home. Well, at least he could keep it as his treasure and look at it whenever he needed to.

He showed it to the fox immediately but was so engrossed in giving the ring loving little rubs to keep it shining he did not wonder at his friend's unusual silence. But that night, after a fine supper of roots and grubs, as he and his friend the fox settled themselves before the entrance to their den to look out onto the sleeping meadow where the moonlight lay like silver upon the flowers and grasses, the fox had his say.

"Dear mole," he began, "from the time I could run my training started. If I were to eat I had to learn and what I had to learn was how to steal. Unluckily I am not like you, able to digest what the earth grows freely. I must have meat. But—and I confess this solely to you who are my heart's comrade—I am sometimes haunted by what I have stolen. Ghost-chickens cluck wildly through my dreams at night. Ghost-rabbits thump through my sleep like drums."

The mole's sympathy was so intense, he too seemed to be hearing the marching rabbits and the taunting chickens.

The fox glanced at his troubled friend. "Oh, do not let my dreams haunt yours," he said. "But you see I have no choice in the matter." He stopped and no further words were spoken.

Yet, to the mole, the silence seemed to be speaking and at last he could answer it. "The ring is not mine," he said slowly. "I must return it."

"If you say so," was the fox's only comment.

"Right now," continued Maybe. "It belongs to the lady."

"I will go with you. You may need protection."

"No," said Maybe. "I must do it by myself. I took it. Now I must untake it."

The fox watched the small, gray shape disappear into the darkness. But he did not re-enter the den. He would wait until his friend came back even if until sunrise.

This time Maybe was carrying the ring on his snout so that he might take last looks at its gleaming loveliness. To do this his eyes had to slightly cross themselves and that was why he tripped over a moving group of gray lumps.

After the alarmed chorus of squeals and squeaks had been sorted out into indignant comments of "Well, some are just born clumsy!" and "You'd think he'd recognize a crowd when it crosses his path!" and one eloquent "By gad!" Maybe saw that he had collided with a gathering of mice.

"Sorry fellows," said the mole, smiling.

They couldn't help smiling back.

"Where are you headed for?" asked Maybe.

"Our Tuesday night campfire," said their leader. "We're the Lady Patrol, you know."

Maybe didn't but he politely did not reveal his ignorance.

"Come with us," suggested one of them.

"Yes, do!"

Since they seemed pointed in the direction of the lady's house the mole decided to follow. This would gain him an entrance into the interior without searching one out. And a few minutes later he was in the parlor, witness to a very odd sight.

Inside the polished brown tile of the fireplace was a mouse-sized bonfire of twigs and dried pine needles and all around in a neat circle sat a ring of wide-eyed mice listening intently to Maybe's acquaintance of the morning. Alfred was speaking on the importance of obedience to his orders, that as master of the house what he said came first.

Both the warmth and the unaccustomed lateness of the hour combined to make the mole somewhat sleepy and it was with shock that he felt someone tampering with his nose.

He jerked backward. The ring tumbled from his snout.

"Thank you," Alfred was saying, "for returning my crown."

"Your crown?" spluttered Maybe, the

sight of the rose ring now atop the rodent's head offending him to anger. "That belongs to the lady and she shall have it. I found it in the orchard where she dropped it."

"I think not," said the leader of the patrol. He had stepped to the farther side of the fire.

The mole advanced on Alfred, his teeth showing, his intent to knock the ring from his head.

"Patrol!" shouted Alfred. "Attack!"

The command was so unexpected the mice forgot their training and scrabbled over and under each other like a wave of gray water toward the mole.

Maybe sat erect and shoveled them out of his way with both paws. He had dug through harder substances than these soft little creatures.

The ones in the rear fell backward into the fire. At the first touch of the heat they leaped frantically in all directions so that for

the next moment there was a scattering of
flaring twigs and tails and sparks showering
from the fireplace.

The Patrol fled so fast, their leader lead-
ing, that they did not even see the hearth
rug smolder into flames in six places. Nor
was there anyone to see the mole, his eyes
tight shut, roll over and over these fiery
spots like a tumbler in a circus without
regard for his singed fur or the pain of the
burns. Stubbornly, his teeth clenched
against the hurting, he rolled backward and

forward until the last flicker was smothered and only tiny drifts of smoke curled up from the rug.

For a long while he lay panting, his breath so short his chest ached. At last with a weary heave he got to his paws. His eyes watered but not only because of the acrid sting of the smoke. The mouse had the ring for a crown and probably tomorrow would, because of it, proclaim himself not master of the house but king of the country. Not that Maybe really cared that the mouse's conceit would be even greater. He would never be cured of that if he lived a thousand years. But that he, Maybe, had failed the lady, the large and generous kindness of her, was more than his control could bear.

His tears cooled his cheeks but his heart still felt the hot arrow of failure.

It was almost morning when Maybe, dragging himself carefully through the rough grasses, approached the den. He was too tired to notice the quick brightening of the fox's eyes as he came in sight or even to be but dimly aware of being supported the last few feet and helped to his corner of the den. He slept out the day.

It was the smell of chicken soup that awoke him and when the two of them had sat down to their supper the mole told the whole sad story.

The fox said nothing until the mole had completed the last dreary sentence. He waited such a long moment to speak he found the mole staring at him. Then he spoke, very solemnly. "Dear Maybe, you did not save the ring. You saved the house."

Maybe leaned back to think. Then, very gradually, as the sky fills with stars one after the other, his thoughts began to shine for him. "So I did," he said softly. "So I did."

And two days from then when he was once more in the orchard, counting apples, he saw the lady. With a basket in her left hand she was picking the first red ones with her right, and there on her finger, glowing gold, was the ring of roses.

Maybe guessed that she must have found it in the mouse's doll house at a moment when Alfred was not wearing it. But however the finding, it was hers again.

The mole stepped out from behind the shadow of the tree he was under and in full sight, as she looked smiling down at him, he bowed.

The Promise

The fox had only been absent for two nights on his autumn tour of near and far relatives when the disturbances began. The first thing the mole became aware of was the unusual quietness of the meadow just outside the den. The small scurries and clickings, the cheeps and the slithers that signaled the movements of the night creatures were so diminished that even the chewing of the rabbits seemed loud. And though the stars could be seen in their places it was as if invisible clouds of darkness hung over the stillness.

Maybe left with his supper only half-eaten. He stood in the entrance to the den looking out. The fox would have known what to make of all this but he was to be gone for many days so it was up to the mole to discover the cause. Otherwise his dreams would be sour and scary.

Was some foreign beast passing through? Had a tiger escaped a circus? Was a plowing machine on the loose with the intent to churn up the earth into chaos?

The mole tried to chuckle at his own ideas but the sound that came from his mouth was squeezed. And the longer he stood there wondering the faster his heart beat. There was only one thing to do. Explore.

Timidly he stepped forth into the open. He pointed his nose upward and breathed in thoughtfully, separating the scents as they came to him. There was no hint of a stranger but the silence had deepened. Now even the rabbits had left the clearing. He walked slowly to the center of the meadow, careful to stay concealed within the clumps of herbs and grasses. He waited. Nothing. No one. He listened, his hearing alert as it had never been before. Only a light wind in the distant trees stirred the air and far off the cackle of a farmyard hen.

He tensed. He must get a better view. His legs a-tremble, he climbed a low boulder.

From here he could see over the surface. But no thing protruded above the motionless landscape. He raised his head.

Suddenly a giant screech, a rush of wings, and two enormous yellow eyes swooped down on him. Steely claws dug into his soft fur and he felt himself lifted higher and higher so fast his breath clogged in his throat.

He called out "Save me! Save me!" and he knew he was calling to the fox. But there was no ready friend below to leap to his rescue. He let himself go limp, hoping it would dislodge the claws that stung into him like prongs of fire. But his captor simply increased his speed, his great, brown wings blanking out the moon and the stars.

With just one glimpse of the blurred earth below Maybe fainted.

When he awoke he didn't believe he was still alive and he pinched himself hard, once and then once again. Then he looked. A round hole in front of him allowed a little light and where he was smelled of pine. He guessed he was inside a tree trunk. Something wiggled from under his stomach and emerged to show itself to be a mouse.

"Whew!" said the tiny brown animal.

"Why didn't it kill us?" asked Maybe, hoping for an explanation.

"We're being saved for later," replied the mouse. "And *it* is an owl. I was humming the first bars of a new song, not paying correct attention to danger, when he caught me. Now," his thready voice broke, "now I'll never get to finish it."

"What a pity," murmured the mole absent-mindedly. He was hunting a means of escape but his mind seemed emptier than an ancient walnut. "How high up are we?" he asked the mouse.

"Too high for me to climb down," answered the dejected creature. "I looked."

"Then it's too high for me to tumble out," said Maybe.

"Much," said the mouse.

"Where's the owl, I wonder," mused the mole.

"Asleep by now," said the mouse surprisingly. "You see, I've been here for three days and I know his habits. He doesn't wake until the next night."

"Then we've got tomorrow."

The mouse shrugged. "For what it's worth, we have it."

"You could finish your song."

The mouse brightened. "So I could. And so I will. Goodnight, mole. It's much cheerier with you here."

"Goodnight," responded Maybe but as for cheer he found none in the stale darkness of his prison.

The next morning as the first rays of the sun leveled into the hole in the tree trunk the mole discovered the mouse gone. For an instant his heart lurched. Even such small company was better than none. Then he heard the humming. The mouse was seated on the nearest branch, his tail wrapped tight around his perch, trying out tunes.

But any pleasure Maybe might have taken in the compositions was immediately cut short by the sight of the gigantic owl on the next branch upward. "Shush!" warned Maybe. He jerked his paw in the direction of their enemy.

The mouse giggled. "Oh, he can't hear you. Deaf as a stone and twice as heavy with sleep."

"All the same," insisted the mole, "I'd stop if I were you. No sense taking chances."

"So would I," came a voice as edged as a knife just above them. "Besides you're off pitch."

The voice descended and became a squirrel, but such a one as Maybe had never seen before. Something like wings were attached from his hind feet to his sides and his tail

was less plumey than the ordinary members
of his family.

"I'm a flyer," the animal explained to
Maybe's questioning eyes.

"Oh," said the mole.

"Oh, indeed!" shrilled the mouse. "Now
I am saved! You can take me off on your
back, restore me to the ground."

"I could if I wished," said the squirrel cooly.

"And me?" asked Maybe. "Me too?"

The squirrel scrutinized the mole all over as though he were a lump of doubtful cheese. "Well, you're a bit heavy. But I expect I *could* manage." He waited for the rise of relief in Maybe's face. "If I wished to," he added slowly, tantalizingly.

"And why don't you wish to?" the mouse demanded. He had learned, small as he was young, that he must take advantage of everything and everyone.

"All efforts must be paid for," said the squirrel.

The mole, remembering the many kindnesses of his friend the fox, gifts and deeds offered and given as freely as trees give their leaves to the autumn wind, did not agree with the squirrel but he said only, "And what do you ask of us in exchange for our rescue?"

"The gathering of a hundred walnuts, no more no less, delivered to my storehouse in the old oak by tomorrow at sunrise."

"Oh my!" protested the mole. He knew the distance between the one walnut tree and the old oak. To carry a hundred nuts, one at a time, would take at least three days, even with the mouse's help.

"That's the bargain," said the squirrel flatly. "It's your life not mine."

The mouse winked at the mole. "Take it," he said and the mole knew from the wink that the mouse, once safe, intended to keep no promises at all. He would have to fulfill the contract alone.

"We'll take it," and as he spoke he released a wordless prayer like a curl of smoke that he might be capable of paying the ransom.

"You first," said the squirrel to the mouse, and the latter had no sooner clutched himself onto the squirrel's back than the flyer,

44

his tail lifted like a rudder, dived downward. He was only two feet above the ground when he braked, rose one foot up, then skidded to a stop. The mouse shakily disappeared into the grasses.

Maybe, watching from the branch, felt he would never see the mouse again. The squirrel returned for the second flight. It took a few minutes to adjust his larger body on top of the squirrel's and the takeoff was so wobbly the two of them almost tumbled headfirst in midair. But at last, with only a bad jolt at the end, they reached the ground.

"Remember," cautioned the squirrel. "Tomorrow at sunrise or—"

"No need to threaten me," said the mole with dignity. "I'll do it."

But after the squirrel had gone the mole burrowed his nose into the warm earth and snuffled the old familiar smells, trying to forget. If only the fox were home! If only he had the cunning and the craft of his companion! If only he weren't just a simple mole, good for digging and not much else!

A crow passed by and the flap of his wings brought the terrible image of the owl so vividly back to him he jerked all over. He must make a start. He hurried to the walnut tree, and shuffling among the fallen leaves, uncovered so many walnuts it only took him an hour to assemble the required hundred.

But when he was finished, his fur pleasantly scented by the green skins, he had only to glance across the meadow and through the fence to the squirrel's oak tree to realize the utter hopelessness of his task. And it was then that the true peril entered his mind. He could take the long journey, nut by nut, all day without pause but what of the night? The owl would capture him on the first nocturnal crossing and this time he knew the monster would eat him on the spot.

He sat upright to savor the peace and fragrance of his country through his nose. It might be for the last time. And the more he sniffed the closer he came to despair. Who was he? What was he? Nothing. A maybe of a mole. The word "mole" seemed to roll like a ball through his thoughts—a hollow ball, for he had almost come to the end of hope.

Then, suddenly, the word sounded very loud inside his head. MOLE. That's what he was! With a thrust so powerful the dirt flew a foot into the air, he began to tunnel. On and on, deeper and deeper, the run a gentle downward slope, its sides as smooth as a pipe.

He paused at noon to eat the grubs he had collected, then went at it again with no slackening of his speed. At dusk he emerged to check his direction and just as his head brushed against the clover above him he saw again the glaring yellow of the owl's eyes and saw his wings spread to sweep up some other small and trembling citizen of the meadow. Maybe ducked downward and continued his labors. He was more than halfway to the squirrel's oak.

At one hour before dawn he was finished. Disregarding his tiredness he raced back through the run to the walnut tree and began the delivery of the nuts. One after the other he threw them into the tunnel and watched them roll downward and when he had counted the full hundred he followed the last of them. But when he arrived at the end he realized he had not planned on one thing—the nuts were banked up, one against the other, with the mole at the tag end and no way for him to get them out unless he exposed himself to the deadly watchfulness of the owl!

He would have to risk it. But before he started to widen the run with legs that ached from the loss of hope, he heard a tiny singing at the outer entrance of his hole where the first walnuts were showing.

"Ho, down there!" came the squeaky tones of the mouse. "Shove as hard as you can while I pile the nuts at the foot of the oak. The squirrel can stow them in his storage hole by himself, lazy thing that he is!"

"Watch out for the owl!" Maybe called back. "I saw him!"

"That's a chance I have to take!" replied the mouse as he heaved the first walnut from the tunnel. "I finished my song, old mole!" he announced between throws. "Want to hear it? I'd better sing it for somebody, just in case."

"Sing away!" Maybe encouraged him, wishing he could do more than just push the chain of nuts up to this courageous little creature.

"Here it is. The Song of the Tail."

With my tail
I flail
The fury
The worry
The ring-around scurry
The underground flurry
Long, sweet and furry
It leads me to glory!

He sang it once. He sang it twice. Then with a pause to ask "Like it, do you?" he sang it a third time. And all during the recital the walnuts churned up from the tunnel and were piled high between the roots of the oak.

As the last six tumbled aboveground the mole among them, a screech to tear open the sky split the silence. Maybe had one glimpse of the great brown wings descending. He dived into the heap of nuts, dragging the mouse with him by his tail. He knew this movable shelter was no shelter at all, that the owl would scoop them both

up into death. He closed his eyes, the mouse beneath him, and waited, shuddering, for the curved claws to cut him to the heart.

Instead, a huge pillow seemed to flop down on him. Instinctively he struggled free of the burden of softness, still pulling the mouse by his tail. He made for the entrance of his run and not until he was almost completely concealed did he dare to peek up and out.

There lay the monster owl, panting for the breath that the fall onto the rolling walnuts had squashed from him. Groggily he rose to a standing position and with one fearful glance around him, flapped his bruised wings until they bore him once more into the air.

A little while later when the two animals were cozily seated in the fox's den, the mole looked into the smaller eyes of the mouse and smiled. "You're a kind of hero, you know," Maybe said a bit shyly.

The mouse nodded and smiled at the mole in his turn with such thankfulness Maybe had to look away. But all the mouse said was, "Saved by my tail, I was. Want to hear my song once more?"

Where the Sun Goes

When the turtle began his journey no one even noticed. It was just the old turtle going somewhere so slowly it made one sleepy to watch him. But when the crow, bored with the clear serenity of the summer day, remarked that for two hours he had not paused, he announced the event in a voice not even the mole, far underground, could escape.

"See the speed king of the country mount the hill! See the dust rise from his whirring feet!" The bird posed himself in front of the turtle. "Where the deuce are you off to, old dear? To circle the earth before supper?"

The turtle widened his lidded eyes and replied with great simplicity. "I am going to see where the sun goes."

The crow cawed rudely. "Well, that's an astonishment, to be sure! Listen everybody where the turtle's going!"

The rabbits lifted their noses from their feeding. The mice sat up straight the better to see. Even the beetles stopped rattling their wings while the butterflies paused in midair.

"He is going to see where the sun goes!" the crow announced for all the world to hear.

A tittering rose from the trees and the meadow in such chorus that the mole shoved up from his tunnel with all speed. What must the poor old turtle be feeling? It wasn't so bad if just one were against you but to have the whole community a part of the ridiculing was too much.

He was able to come up out of the ground just ahead of the turtle. He smiled and said "Good morning." The turtle only nodded and kept on lifting one leg after the other in slow motion, obviously not intending to pause for a moment of chat.

"It would have been better," continued

the mole kindly, now keeping pace with the turtle, "if you had said you were going to visit your cousin for tea or that you had an errand at the bottom of the hill."

"But I'm not and I didn't," said the turtle briefly.

The mole sighed. This was not a lively mind.

By now the crow had worked up the tittering to strangled giggles by such remarks as "He's quick as mud, the silly old dud" and "Any bets he gets there before the sun sets?" and many others.

A very bold rat darted out from nowhere and plopped a rotten tomato onto the center of his shell where it dripped seeds down his sides. A blue jay swooped down and attached a trailing vine to his tail. A mouse hopped onto one of the leaves and rode it like a raft, calling out as he skidded inch by inch across the grass, "I'm off to the races!"

"We're not far from my den," said the mole. "Stop in and we'll clean you off and give you something to drink."

The turtle only wobbled his head to mean "no" and lumbered up the slope, seeming not to care. But as the mole looked intently into the corner of his lidded right eye he saw a bead of moisture that might have been a tear.

Suddenly Maybe's patience cracked wide open and with both paws he scraped off the tomato, ripped away the vine, and gave the mouse a hearty cuff on both ears. Getting behind the turtle he rapped twice on his shell, causing the turtle's legs and head to retreat inward. Bracing himself for a forward thrust, the mole shoved the body of the turtle straight ahead foot after foot until at last he was placed inside the mole's home.

"You can come out now," said the mole. "You're safe."

Cautiously the turtle poked out his nose

and then his eyes. "But I'm not where I want to be," he said.

"No, that's true. You're where I want you to be. I couldn't stand any more of that cruel teasing."

The turtle waved his forelegs and gradually began to turn in the direction of the entrance to the den. "I want to see where the sun goes," he said and swiveled himself into a position of leaving.

"Wait for just one question!" the mole requested, a tone of pleading deepening his voice.

"I will," said the turtle.

"Do you know where the sun goes down?"

"I did when I started," answered the turtle stolidly. "Before you came between me and it."

"And now you don't."

"And now I don't."

"Then stay here until it begins to lower

and then we can see." The mole privately hoped that his friend the fox would be back by then and would solve the situation, saving the turtle's pride.

For reply the turtle simply pulled in his head and appeared to go to sleep.

But although the mole deprived himself of all his daily pleasures in order to keep watch for the fox's homecoming, there was no sight of his cinnamon shape or sound of his happy bark as he crossed the rise of the hill. And now it was too late to attend his arrival any longer for the sun was lowering and in all honor the turtle must be alerted.

The dozing animal responded immediately, if slowly, to the mole's tap, tap on his shell. He gazed straight into the round, orange blaze of the sun and once more his legs inched him forward.

Maybe groaned. He would never make it anywhere, this dear, stupid creature, just go on and on until his strength faded, until his perfect stubbornness brought him to his last sleep.

Well, he could at least keep him company on his final journey. So Maybe shuffled along beside the hardly-moving turtle, suppressing his impatience by humming a few songs he had learned from the wind.

He was scarcely through the third tune when he was startled into silence by a peculiar series of inner grunts coming from the turtle's throat. His head was stretched full length from his shell. Maybe looked where he was looking and there, far in front of them, was the house of the miserable Mr. Sting, and behind it was the sun. It's windows were afire with light.

The mole gulped. If the turtle ever appeared at that person's door he would find himself popped into a pot and become turtle soup.

"I have found it," said the turtle.

The mole tried to laugh but only achieved a kind of gurgle. "But you'll never get there by nightfall," he said. "Best to turn back."

"If not tonight, tomorrow," stated the turtle.

For an instant the mole felt the chill of desperation shudder through his body. He was only safe by daylight. Who knew what peril of claw and beak would pounce down on him? Then he dug his paws into the earth and called out to the paling sky for courage. How could he possibly divert this bull-headed creature from ending up in a pot of boiling water? Then, from somewhere, like a spring in the desert, came an idea.

He turned to the turtle. "I'll get you there if you'll trust me."

"I do," said the turtle who had never even met the mole before this day.

The mole quickly chewed off four tall, tough grasses, tied them together into a harness and fastened it around the turtle's shell. "Now you must pull yourself in and stay there until I tell you to come out."

The turtle obeyed.

Maybe roped the free end of the harness around his own shoulders and began to pull. The turtle came easily for the first few hundred yards because the ground was smooth. It was like dragging a heavy sled. But there were many yards still to go and the time of the owl was very near. Already the sun had half sunk behind the horizon. Maybe even wished that the turtle's former tormentors would join them. They might have been able to help. But there was only the first whistling of the night wind like a ghost

in his ears and its chill fingers ruffling his fur.

He pulled harder. Now small stones slipped and slid under his paws. But he kept his goal steadily before him—the house of the lady. She would adopt the turtle gladly as she had so many other homeless or discontented beings of the woods and meadows. And the turtle would never know the difference. A house was a house. He would believe the sun set inside hers forever.

He struggled on, fear pushing him, hope pulling.

He had just reached the border of the lady's vegetable garden and was about to drop the harness, bid the turtle goodbye, and flee, when a vicious hissing and spitting confronted him. It was a cat!

The mole dodged the first strike of her extended claws but the second caught him under his right leg. He shrieked, high and wild.

Suddenly a hollow voice called out to him. "Get behind me and dig!" It was the turtle who had reared himself on his hind legs like a shield.

Maybe scrambled around this protection, narrowly escaping a blow to his eyes. The cat howled and arched his back, his tail a rod of fury.

The mole plunged his head into the ground and worked his powerful paws like twin shovels, left, right, left, right, until he had entirely buried himself under a head of cabbage.

The turtle flopped flat again. The cat, realizing he had somehow lost his prey, sang such a series of enraged screeches that a window opened and then a door and in two minutes the lady stood above him.

"Stop that!" she ordered the cat.

Then she saw what she believed to be the cause. "But you foolish creature," she admonished the cat. "It's only a turtle! He is welcome in our garden for as long as he wishes to stay. Come back to the house and I'll give you some cream to quiet your temper."

She picked up the still bristling animal and spoke to the turtle. "I hope to find you here tomorrow."

And so she did, for the rest of the turtle's life. He had completed his quest. And each evening at sunset he would remember where the sun goes when it sets, into the parlor of the kind lady.

When the mole made his way back to his den early the next morning after his night in hiding, the fox had returned and it took a long time to explain what had happened.

The Last Hunt

The morning was deep into autumn, the trees flaring high in their scarlet and gold leaves, the frosted air pungent with the sweetness of mold. Just to breathe made Maybe laugh as he stepped from the den to sun himself.

"Feeling it, are you?" asked the fox, just behind him.

"Feeling what?" asked the mole, knowing exactly what his friend meant but wanting a word for it.

"The joy."

Maybe nodded, smiling.

"Want to pay a visit to an old friend?" said the fox casually, but the mole heard the importance of the question. "It will mean a long hike but I will be your horse."

The mole saw that the fox had strapped a bag of provisions onto his back. "Gladly," said Maybe. "But where are we going?"

"To pass an hour or two with an old enemy of mine, the great hunting hound."

Maybe looked his surprise.

The fox laughed. "Yes, we shared so many hunts together, he chasing, me fleeing, neither ever winning, that finally when he retired from his job as leader of the hounds we just naturally became friends."

The mole, who had learned never to question the fox's eccentricities for they always turned out to be some part of wisdom, climbed up to his place behind the fox's shoulders and called out, "Let's go!"

So the fox went at an easy trot through the entire morning of fields and streams and brilliant woods until at last he arrived at a length of white fence so long the mole could see no end to it.

"Here we are," said the fox and the mole slid down to the ground, content to stretch and roll for a moment in the clipped grass.

The fox barked three times, then again, and there from behind the fence appeared the noble shape of a hound who, in spite of aging jowls and a slightly grayed hide, would have been acknowledged an aristocrat in any royal pack.

The two animals bowed to each other, then relaxed into a kind of simple frolic, feigning affectionate blows with their paws. Next the fox introduced his two friends and they all three sat down and began to catch up on the events of their separate worlds.

"Retirement really isn't too boring," said the hound in response to the fox's interest. "I'm particularly pleased not to be forced to corner any more foxes." He smiled widely.

"You were always more than fair," commented the fox. "In fact several times you gave me the advantage."

"Did I now?" said the hound. "Perhaps. But such things never got back to the Master of the Hunt. I saw to it. Had tight control over the others."

"What was behind your kindness?" asked

the fox. "You were certainly not trained in that direction."

The massive dog looked into the fox's eyes. "Respect," he replied.

The fox's tail switched with pleasure. "Let's have a run, shall we?" he said to cover his embarrassment. "Show the mole how we did it?"

Maybe climbed back into his place as rider. "Hang on tight!" instructed the fox and he loped swiftly into the nearest cover of trees.

The hound did not move.

"He'll give me a good head-start," explained the fox, increasing his pace until, soon, even the fences were out of sight.

But a few minutes later the mole wondered why the fox halted and glanced back, his eyes puzzled. Then he worked his way out of the trees and ascended a hill. But nowhere in the now visible distance was a glimpse of the tawny approach of the hound. Instead there came the far-off sound of a horn.

The fox quivered. "The hunt!" he exclaimed, shock a rasp in his voice. "They're off and away!"

Now like an accompaniment to the blazened notes they could hear the pack baying.

"Let's go home," murmured the mole. But the fox remained motionless, listening with an alertness the mole had never witnessed before in his friend. It was as if his ears and mind were sorting out all the most minute movements of the countryside.

"They're heading toward us," he said to the mole. "I must run. I will leave you in a safe place, and if I can, come back for you. If not you must return by yourself. Do not wait beyond dusk."

"No," said Maybe. "I will stay with you, no matter what." He clenched his paws more firmly in the fox's ruff and did not speak again. The fox was within a concentration so intense he seemed to have forgotten the mole. He had to.

The noise of the hounds was nearer now and with a high bound the fox dived back into the shelter of the woods. He began to run in a zig-zag pattern. Once he splashed a hundred yards through a stream and paused to rest on the far bank. His breathing was shorter and Maybe could feel his muscles quiver.

Perhaps he delayed a little too long. Perhaps he was out of practice. For, like a tangle of thunder, the pack broke through the trees downstream and checked their pursuit, sniffling and snuffling, trying to recapture the scent. And at that instant Maybe saw the great hound bringing up the rear. He was lunging ferociously at the rear leg muscles of the other dogs, biting where he could, ignoring the snarling attacks of the younger hounds. Maybe realized he was trying to stop the hunt. The old dog's chest was bleeding from the resistance of the others.

Then as if to dispose of this fierce inter-ference, the lead hound signaled a mass charge and each one wheeled about-face, formed a tight circle and stood against their former leader, teeth bared, their throats heavy with growling.

The fox said one word, "Goodbye," and barked so sharply the mole's ears rang.

As if reversed by a giant wind, the hounds swiveled and in one wave poured toward the fox, leaving the hound alone and unable to save his friend.

Suddenly the mole felt as though he were in the eye of a cyclone so fast did the fox skim the ground. He later had a vague re-membrance of being carried through an or-chard, of ducking through the doors of a vast barn and out again, scattering chickens and pigs like dust, of another wild circling through trees and thickets that tore little scratches in his skin. He sensed, his eyes shut, his paws just barely holding on, the

terrible ordeal of the fox and he could feel
the pounding of his heart all the way up
through his backbone. But all the mole
could do was to become all one small force
of love and faith for his friend, to have a

kind of senseless trust that they would get to him and somehow help.

Abruptly the terror of the hounds vanished, the flight halted, and the mole smelled the sweetness of the den all around him. He tumbled off the fox's back. The fox lay flat and barely breathing on the warm, earthen floor. Quickly the mole brought him water on a leaf and put it under his nose. The fox lapped awkwardly at the cooling liquid but his eyes opened.

The mole couldn't seem to stop patting the fox's head as if he might suddenly become unreal and not be there at all.

The fox tried to smile but he was too exhausted. But he could whisper. "Maybe," he said very low, "we're home."

"And you saved not just me and you," said the mole, "but the hound as well."

"I had to," said the fox. "They would have killed him and besides—" His voice drifted into silence.

"Besides what?" prompted the mole gently. "Why?"

The fox raised his head and there reappeared in his eyes a kind of light that reminded Maybe of the morning star.

"Respect," said the fox and lay back to welcome sleep.

JULIA CUNNINGHAM has won wide recognition as the author of *Dorp Dead, Macaroon, Candle Tales, Burnish Me Bright, Far in the Day,* and *The Treasure is the Rose,* a 1973 National Book Award nominee. Born in Spokane, Washington, Miss Cunningham attended a variety of schools from New York to Virginia, but considers herself self-educated. After a journeyman's experience of jobs, a year in France led to becoming a real writer and to publication. She now lives in Santa Barbara, California, where she works in a bookstore when she is not busy writing.

CYNDY SZEKERES is well-known for her captivating animal characters. She has illustrated over thirty picture books, including *Pippa Mouse* and *Moon Mouse,* an AIGA award-winner. She is also the creator of the popular *Cyndy's Animal Calendars* and *Cyndy's Workbook Diary.*

She lives on a farm in Vermont with her husband, Gennaro Prozzo, a graphic artist, and their children, Marc and Chris.

FIC
CUN

C. 2

Cunningham, Julia

Maybe, a mole

DATE DUE	SEP 2 6 1990		
DEC. 3 1986 GRI			
JAN 28 1987 8LA			
NOV 24 1987			
DEC 02 1987 You			
JAN 1 3 1988			
FEB 0 3 1988			
MAR 0 2 1988 JAN 2 '90			
JAN 3 '89 MAY 0 2 1990			
JAN 24 '89			
DEC 4 '89			
DEC 11 '89			

no card